Dear Stacy,
I pray this
reminder to you that as a child of
God, you have a good & godly purpose.
Iris Carignan
4/21/19

MORIAH'S WINGS

Happy Resurrection
Day

IRIS CARIGNAN

Illustrations by Iris Carignan

Cover Design by Chautona Havig

All scripture quoted is the King James Version and public domain.

First Printing Edition March 2019

Celebrate Lit Publishing

www.celebratelitpublishing.com/

ISBN 13: 978-0-9995370-6-0

I dedicate this book to all of my grandchildren and especially to my granddaughter Ella who inspired the illustrations. I give thanks to my Lord who inspired the story through His word and the prompting of His Holy Spirit. May each child, big or small, gain a sense of God's purpose in their own life through the reading of it.

CHAPTER ONE

LONG AGO IN a land far away, there was a young girl of little acclaim, and Despairity was her name. She lived with her mother and brothers in a remote corner of Israel, and they were very poor. Even though her name was given out of great despair, she was a hopeful and bright child. It was as if her troubling name was the challenge that made this child stronger and more determined.

There came a day, however, that nearly broke her spirit—a hot and thirsty day, when a band of men from a land named Aram passed by her home. She was cheerfully doing her chores, a heavy load of sticks balanced atop her head. Yet, it didn't slow her happy skip from the thicket of trees towards her house. A caravan of camels, mules, and men came to a sudden stop right in front of their family well. Believing the men had stopped to give water to their animals, she wasn't afraid, even as they came closer and closer.

Despairity bent over to drop the load of sticks next to the pile she'd been gathering all day. As she leaned over, something in the dirt caught her eye. "There you are, Tikva," she said, brushing off

the soiled and ragged doll. "You must have fallen out of my sash this morning."

Then, as she straightened back up, a large hand suddenly grabbed her arm and jerked her away. Despairity screamed, and her mother Hannah came running out of the house.

"No-o-o-o!" Hannah shrieked as two men lifted Despairity into a wagon and tied her hands together. "Please don't take my only daughter, my joy!"

But they cracked their whips and rushed the caravan away. Hannah ran frantically alongside, begging and pleading for mercy from the men, but she couldn't keep up with their fast getaway. Gasping for breath, she stopped in defeat and shouted a last goodbye to her daughter.

"May Jehovah be your hope and protection!" she hollered through hot tears.

Despairity thought she heard her mother say something else too; something about being free and about butterflies.

With each dusty, bumpy measure of road leading further away from home, Despairity's fear and anxiousness grew. She knew that things had changed forever, yet she did not cry or even whimper. Although a life of poverty had been hard, it was what she knew, what she expected. How would the strangers treat her, and would she ever be free? The rope around her wrists had been loosed many miles back, but her heart felt more and more captive.

Still clutching her doll, Despairity lifted it to her face. "Don't worry, Tikva," she said. "I will keep you safe." And with that, she pressed the doll to her cheek, hugging it tightly. Tikva meant "hope," and this tattered doll of cloth and straw would be her only tangible connection to home.

Despairity lost track of how many days they had traveled, but sensed they were no longer in Israel. Along the journey, four more children—all older than her—had also been captured. Finally, it seemed the journey was over. The camels and wagons came to a halt in a city named Aram, also known as Syria. The children were ordered out and told to stand in the center of a courtyard. A small crowd quickly gathered around as the young captives stood shaking in fear.

Despairity was very tired, hungry, and thirsty, but she stood among them with her head held high. One by one, the other captives were led away by strangers. Each time, the clinking sound of coins rang out the toll of slavery. She closed her eyes, hoping it would all go away. *Maybe it was just a bad dream*, she told herself. Instead of calming her, shutting away sight only seemed to magnify every sound and smell that attached itself to the day.

Opening her eyes again, she blinked at the hot, wavy images rising from the stone pavement. Then, out of the dust and distorted haze, she saw an image that looked like a beautiful young woman. Was it a mirage? Despairity blinked again. The image grew clearer. She saw a sheer blue scarf draped around the lady's head and her tunic of white, blue, and lavender was tied at the waist with a purple sash.

Then, out of nowhere, a clear yet strange thought came to Despairity. It was so strong she dared not ignore it. *Offer to water the animals*, came the commanding thought. So she walked over to the camels and mules and reached out for the reins of one. She politely asked her captors if she could give the animals some water. Stunned at her unexpected request, the men agreed, and together they led the animals to a nearby well.

As she walked towards the well, she heard the lady ask: "How much for the girl?"

Assuming she was talking about the older girl who was still standing in the courtyard, the men called out a high price.

"No!" she said, pointing towards Despairity. "That girl."

"Oh, you can have her for half the price, but we can offer the other one for a little less if that pleases you," he offered.

"I want the little one." With that she handed over a small bag of coins.

One of the men untied Despairity's hands and ordered her to go with the lady. "You belong to her now," he bellowed.

But Despairity stood frozen in fear and staring in bewilderment. Her emotions suddenly teamed together and pulled against her. Fear and worry about the fate that loomed ahead now held her more captive than any rope could. *Why had Jehovah God let this happen?* she wondered in silent grief.

"Are you deaf, child?" the lady yelled. "Come here. Now!"

Despairity opened her mouth to respond, but nothing would

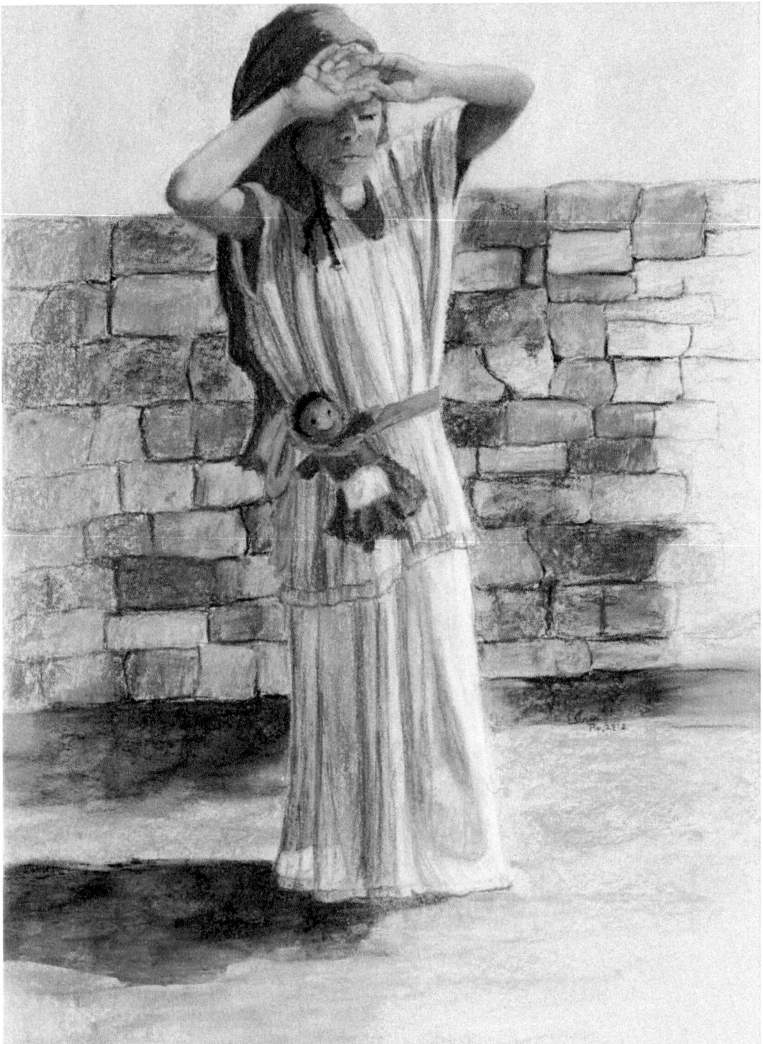

come out. In her mind she was screaming with all her might, but no sound escaped her mouth. Then, as if a protective bubble surrounded her and sealed out any unwanted noise or danger, Despairity did something odd. She lifted her doll and started apologizing.

"I'm so sorry, Tikva. I didn't mean for you to get captured.

Please forgive me. Please, please!" And that's when the dam of determination finally broke.

Her feelings gave way to sobs that poured from every part of her being. Tears streamed down her young cheeks. Then, as if those tears fell into the well of the lady's heart, a softened, caring expression washed across the woman's face. She drew close to Despairity and spoke gently. "What is your name, child?" she asked.

"Despairity. Mara Despairity," she managed to reply.

Bending down to the girl's eye level, the lady tenderly lifted Despairity's quivering chin.

"Little girl of bitter despair, today I give you a new name. From here on you will be called Moriah Asha."

Moriah was a huge name to live up to, because it meant "chosen of God" and was the name of a mountain, too. Asha meant "hope." Both were a strong contrast to Mara Despairity— "Bitter Despair." In the coming days, she did her best to fulfill her name's meaning, but it felt like a pair of sandals three sizes too big. Only time would tell.

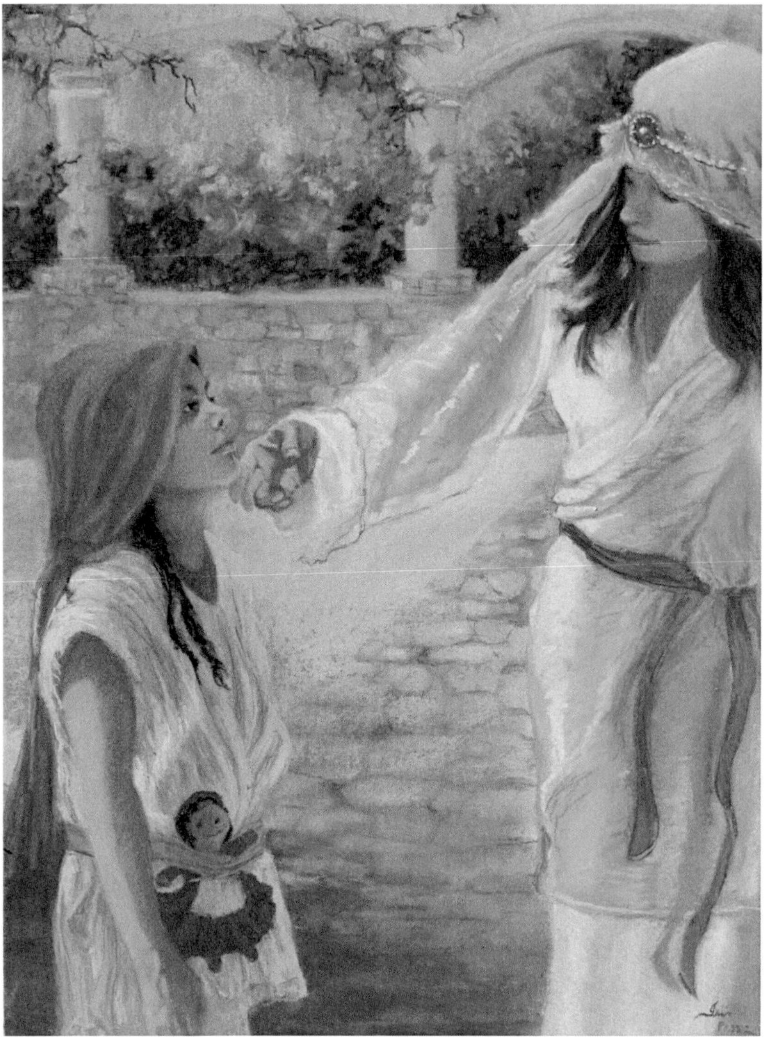

CHAPTER TWO

THE NEXT FEW weeks were filled with lots of chores and many new customs that Moriah had to learn. Adapting to these new ways was more difficult than the hard work. There was so much to learn about manners, customs, and expectations, but she caught on quickly. She served with a cheerful attitude, despite the sadness that pulled on her heart. She missed her family so much, but something her mother used to say had always seemed to help her no matter how hard the problem was.

"Remember child, 'The light of the eyes rejoiceth the heart (Proverbs 15:30a).'"

As the days and months melted into one another, Moriah learned that she could still have a measure of joy within by approaching each day and each task with a prayer and a smile, no matter how she felt inside. And somehow the smile on her face seemed to drift down into her spirit a little more each time.

Her new mistress, Priscilla, was married to a man of great importance. His name was Naaman, and he was a brave soldier. The king of Aram had appointed him as commander over his army. Moriah learned that God had favored Naaman and allowed him to win several important battles. Because of these victories, he was highly regarded by the king. This explained why he and Priscilla lived in a beautiful and spacious home with so many servants.

At the end of every day, Moriah retreated to the tent she shared with the other servant girls. It was a simple tent, but she had her own corner mat to rest on.

She reached for her only treasured connection to home—Tikva—and said a prayer for her family, whom she missed so much. She wondered what her mother would think about her new name and what she might be doing. Maybe she was painting another beautiful design on one of the pieces of wood Moriah had collected for her. Perhaps her mother had even been able to sell some of her painted carvings. Thinking about such things helped Moriah not to feel as sad.

One night, as Moriah began her usual evening prayers, she pulled the doll snugly to her cheek, only this time she noticed an unusual scratchiness. She examined the doll curiously, looking for what might be causing it. Then she noticed a tiny corner of paper sticking out from the doll's ragged pocket. Moriah carefully pulled out the thread that held this mysterious treasure captive. As she held the unfolded piece of paper up to her candle-lit space, a spark of curious hope seemed to ignite her spirit with wonder. The other slave girls giggled mischievously.

"What does it say?" they teased.

"I think it's God's word," she replied confidently.

Laughing wildly at the idea of any slave girl having the slightest learning and knowledge, they all danced in a circle around Moriah singing a song of ridicule.

"Moriah is a mountain, Moriah is a mountain."

Moriah is a mountain, a mountain of lies. Ashes, ashes all fall down."

This mean-spirited teasing hurt Moriah's feelings and pierced

9

her delicate young armor. She may have seemed especially strong for a nine-year-old, but this additional layer of rejection from her own peers stung like a swarm of bees.

"What is all the hilarity and loud clanging I hear?" came their mistress' voice. She peeked into their tent, then entered with irritation spread across her face. "What's going on in here?" she demanded.

"Your favored servant thinks she can read, oh most high

mistress," one girl said. And bowing down low to the ground, they pretended to show honor and respect for Priscilla. Yet, they only hoped to hide their smirking faces from her.

"She has a piece of papyrus paper with words on it," another girl explained further.

"Well, let me see this piece of entertainment so that I can be enlightened as well," Lady Priscilla demanded.

Timidly handing the folded message to her mistress, little Moriah slowly lowered her head with a humble, yet pleading glance. There were few, if any, women in that day who could read, Priscilla was one. She had been blessed with a husband of honor, and Naaman's appointment as commander of the King's army brought certain benefits to their household, including the privilege of learning to read. Priscilla had often glanced over her husband's shoulder as he struggled to learn letters and their meaning. It wasn't long before they both were able to read. This became a secret joy they shared together and united them like a wax seal holding two scrolls together.

Priscilla held the paper up to the lamp in her hand and read aloud.

> *Bless the Lord, O my soul: and all that is within me,*
> *bless his holy name.*
> *Bless the Lord, O my soul, and forget not all his*
> *benefits:*
> *Who forgiveth all thine iniquities; who healeth all thy*
> *diseases;*
> *Who redeemeth thy life from destruction; who*
> *crowneth thee with lovingkindness and tender*
> *mercies;*
> *Who satisfieth thy mouth with good things; so that thy*
> *youth is renewed like the eagle's.*
> *Psalm 103:1-5*

"This is very interesting," Priscilla proclaimed. "Where did you get this?"

Moriah looked squarely into the eyes of her mistress and said proudly, "It was sewn into my doll's pocket. My mother must have put it there for me."

"Well," Priscilla went on, "it is time for all of you to sleep. We have much work tomorrow, and I need you to be well-rested by dawn."

Of course, Moriah lay wide-awake instead. Long after the candle's glow flickered out and the chirping crickets grew silent, her eyes refused to rest. She just couldn't stop thinking about the note. What could it mean? Why did her mother put it there, and how would its discovery affect her service to Mistress Priscilla? Would Jehovah God take her terrible situation as a slave and turn it into something good and purposeful? All of these questions circled around and around in her head all night long.

Just as the night warbler began singing his last good-byes to the night, Moriah finally drifted off to sleep. A dream came vividly just before dawn. It was a colorful and clear vision of a garden with beautiful trees and flowers next to a stream of water. A little yellow butterfly flitted by and beckoned her to follow. Then she saw a holy man walking through the garden. He stopped and reached his hand down into the muddy stream, dipping it seven times. The yellow butterfly flew by again, and a joyous feeling of lightness swept over her. Then the dream was over.

"Get up. Get up." A loud voice interrupted her sweet slumber. It was the voice of the oldest servant girl, Sabrina. Moriah felt someone shake her shoulder as she pried open her sleepy eyes. Her mistress stared back at her.

"Oh! My lady Priscilla," she said, quickly jumping up from her mat. "Forgive me, my lady," she begged earnestly. "I did not intend to sleep so late and am fully ready to serve in any way you wish." Bowing over and over, she pleaded with her mistress.

"Please give me your commands for the day, that I might fulfill your wishes promptly."

"Come into my room now, Moriah Asha!" Lady Priscilla ordered sternly.

All of the other servants glanced at one another with sly expressions. *Would Moriah be punished for this? Would this little Jewish girl get what she deserved instead of the favoritism they had noticed with jealousy?*

Moriah followed her mistress into a beautiful room. She and the other servants had never been allowed in it before. Amazingly, she did not feel fearful or anxious. Then she noticed that her mistress had a very long and sad face. Her shoulders seemed to carry an invisible weight.

"Is something troubling you, my lady?" Moriah asked timidly.

"Yes," she answered sadly.

"If it pleases my lady," Moriah asked shyly, "may I brush your beautiful hair?"

Then, blushing with embarrassment at her own boldness, Moriah stuttered, "I-I," she began, "I used to brush my mother's hair whenever she was sad or discouraged."

"Why, that would be wonderful," Lady Priscilla agreed.

Moriah lifted the silver-handled brush from her mistress' side table and began stroking Priscilla's long black hair. Each gentle gesture seemed to massage her mistress' troubled spirit and relax her slumped shoulders.

After several minutes of silence, Priscilla began her story of woe.

"My husband is very ill," she began. "He has sores on his body, and we think it may be leprosy. If the king finds out, he may have Naaman killed, for he is a harsh man. It is only a matter of time before my husband's illness will be evident, and I am worried beyond hope for all of us."

Just as she finished revealing her worry, Naaman entered the room. Moriah gently laid the brush back on the table. Then, with surprising impulse, she boldly offered advice to her mistress. "If my lord Naaman would seek help from the prophet Elisha, I know that he would be healed," she said.

"Where is this prophet? How do we find him?" Naaman asked.

"He is in Samaria," Moriah replied.

Then Naaman went to the king and told him what the servant girl had said. The king gave him permission to go and seek help from Elisha. He even sent a letter to the king of Israel on his behalf. **"And he departed, and took with him ten talents of silver, and six thousand pieces of gold, and ten changes of raiment." (II Kings 5:5b)**

CHAPTER THREE

MORIAH AND HER mistress could hardly wait for Naaman to return. It had been several days since he left for Samaria, and with each day their concern and excitement grew. During that long wait, Priscilla called Moriah to her room every day, and they shared their thoughts and fears with each other. Sometimes Priscilla gave Moriah motherly advice and instructions on life. Sometimes Moriah's precocious wisdom and spiritual knowledge flowed out upon her mistress like a soothing balm. Priscilla began daily lessons of teaching Moriah how to read, and together they pondered further the meaning of the papyrus note found on her doll. Brushing Priscilla's hair became a regular and special time they both looked forward to.

The other servant girls, except for Sabrina, continued to bully Moriah with lies and rumors of their master's demise. "We heard the king of Israel killed Naaman because of the letter that was sent with him," they claimed. "I heard that he drowned in a muddy river," one girl said. The gossip went on and on. Only one, Sabrina, stayed quiet. She had grown in respect for her younger peer, and they were quickly becoming friends through it all.

Finally Sabrina spoke up in Moriah's defense. "It's better to bite your tongue than to eat your words."

When the day came for Naaman's return, hundreds of people gathered to greet him, some in skeptical curiosity. Would he return as a restored and healthy man? The anxious momentum grew, its intensity like the rising desert sun.

Musicians played. Tambourines jingled and horns blew a resounding fanfare as they saw his approaching caravan. For several days they had heard the distant sound of donkeys braying to one another. It could mean only one thing: a caravan of travelers was coming. The crowd's excitement grew to a rousing fervor, and soldiers formed a pathway of protection for their commander.

The servant girls were not allowed to join the welcoming crowds, and Sabrina noticed Moriah's disappointment. Motioning silently, Sabrina beckoned Moriah to follow her.

"Come on," Sabrina whispered. "I know of a good and safe place where we can watch everything."

And with that, they both snuck away. They perched on top of a tall hill and watched with excited anticipation. There, Sabrina took the opportunity to ask Moriah what she thought would happen and why she had so much confidence as a young girl. They shared some of their fears and sorrows with each other, and Moriah explained her personal story of faith. Sabrina also told her that their mistress, Priscilla, had a special love for Moriah. "I think it's because you remind her of the daughter she lost two years ago." Moriah's heart was immediately humbled. She felt sad as well as blessed with this new understanding. Might not her own mother have felt such a loss when she was captured? It became a wonderful few moments of quiet testimony and bonding.

The sun had begun rising when they spotted a few donkeys on the distant road that weaved its way between the mountains. Then they saw a caravan crest the last hill beyond the valley.

"Look, there he is!" Sabrina shouted and pointed.

They both gasped as they recognized their master Naaman riding his horse in lead. They saw the king and his men approach Naaman and surround him for a time, but they couldn't see well enough to know if their master was restored from his ailment or not.

The caravan came closer as it entered the town, and hordes of people rushed toward it. Soldiers held the crowd back in protection of their leader. From their hilltop perspective they could see the king motion to Priscilla, and she appeared to move towards her husband hesitantly. She bowed respectfully to the king, then to her husband, Naaman. Slowly raising her head, Priscilla's gaze fell on her husband's face, and she reached out to grasp his hands. Then, with excitement and joy she could no longer contain, she let out a yelp.

"He is healed!" she cried out.

The crowd broke into loud cheers of celebration. Even the solemn soldiers raised their swords in salute and whooped happily for their commander.

"He is restored, he is restored!" they all sang out in unison.

The two girls stood with hands raised, praising God in jubilation, then scurried back down the hill before anyone would notice their absence.

Moriah barely made it back to her tent before Naaman summoned her to Priscilla's room.

"Come here," he said, his voice commanding, yet gleeful.

Moriah approached Naaman, then bowed all the way to the floor in honor, respect, and humbled joy for her master. "My lord, the Lord Jehovah has been merciful and good to you and to all of your household."

"Moriah, child, this day I have returned a whole man, and I thank you for sending me to Elisha, God's servant."

"May God's name be praised, O master," she replied. "And, if it pleases my lord, will you share your story with us?"

"Yes, I will. Here, this is for you," he said, handing her a wrapped package. "My wife has told me of your comforting actions and how you have brought joy and hope into our home."

"Oh, most gracious lord!" Moriah gushed as she untied the blue ribbon that held together the wrapping. It was a beautiful hairbrush with hand painted flowers adorning its handle and back.

She cradled it to her breast brimming with gratefulness.

"May this small token of my gratitude be a reminder of God's brushstrokes of love and hope in our lives," Naaman declared in a prophetic tone.

They sat together on Priscilla's rug as Naaman began telling them all that had happened during his journey. He told of how the king of Israel was very troubled at first when he'd read the letter from their king.

He recalled his own dismay and anger at Elisha when he had been instructed to just **"Go and wash in Jordan seven times, and thy flesh shall come again to thee, and thou shalt be clean." (II Kings 5:10b)** At that point Moriah suddenly recalled the dream she'd had the evening before her first visit to Priscilla's bedroom. All of its joyous colors and symbols of hope came flooding back to her memory.

"That's what it meant!" she squealed.

"What *what* meant?" They asked in puzzlement.

"The dream," she said, and then told of the garden and butterfly and seeing the sandals of a holy man leading her somewhere. "Then the holy man dipped his hand in a river seven times," she said excitedly.

"Amazing!" Naaman exclaimed. "Surely Jehovah is God. Moriah Asha, your name truly fits you."

"The papyrus note!" Priscilla suddenly exclaimed. She darted to her bedside table and held up the note that Moriah had found in her doll. "See what it says here," she said, holding it up to the morning light. A look of revelation flashed across her smiling face as she read it once more:

> *Bless the Lord, O my soul: and all that is within me,*
> *bless his holy name.*
> *Bless the Lord, O my soul, and forget not all his*
> *benefits:*
> *Who forgiveth all thine iniquities; who healeth all thy*
> *diseases;*
> *Who redeemeth thy life from destruction; who*
> *crowneth thee with lovingkindness and tender*
> *mercies;*
> *Who satisfieth thy mouth with good things; so that thy*
> *youth is renewed like the eagle's.*
> *Psalm 103:1-5*

The rest of the day was filled with stories from Naaman recounting all his adventures in Samaria. Priscilla and Moriah sat at his feet soaking it all in. The king held a bountiful banquet in honor of the returned and restored commander and Moriah Asha was allowed to attend as a guest.

On this night, Priscilla brushed and braided Moriah's hair and tied the blue ribbon at the top. Then she gave her a matching shawl for her shoulders and shoes that had once belonged to her daughter. As they went out to join the festivities, Moriah caught her reflection in the courtyard pond.

She stood for a long time in stunned revelation of her own beauty.

As the day drew to a close and Moriah settled into her tent, thoughts of the day swirled in her head like dancing fireflies. She gathered her new treasure, the brush, along with her doll and held them up to the candle light.

"Isn't it beautiful?" she told Tikva.

Then, as she looked more closely at the brush, she noticed something. There, painted at the center of the flowers, was a yellow butterfly like the one in her dream. Suddenly, she realized that the style of design was just like her mother's paintings. She closely examined the carved shape of the brush and the kind of wood it was made of. Could it possibly be one of her mother's handmade crafts? She recalled how much her mother always loved butterflies and remembered hearing her mother say something about butterflies the day she was captured.

Moriah suddenly felt joy rising within her, like a breeze lifting the wings of a butterfly. She may never be loosed from slavery, yet Jehovah had set her free from the dark cocoon that held her spirit captive. God had given her a special purpose in life by allowing her to lead Naaman and Priscilla to God's grace and mercy. The brush in her hand was a tangible sign of God's love that gave her hope. She knew in her heart that she would see her mother again one day.

Sleep fell upon her easily that night as a song rose in her heart like a lullaby of love.

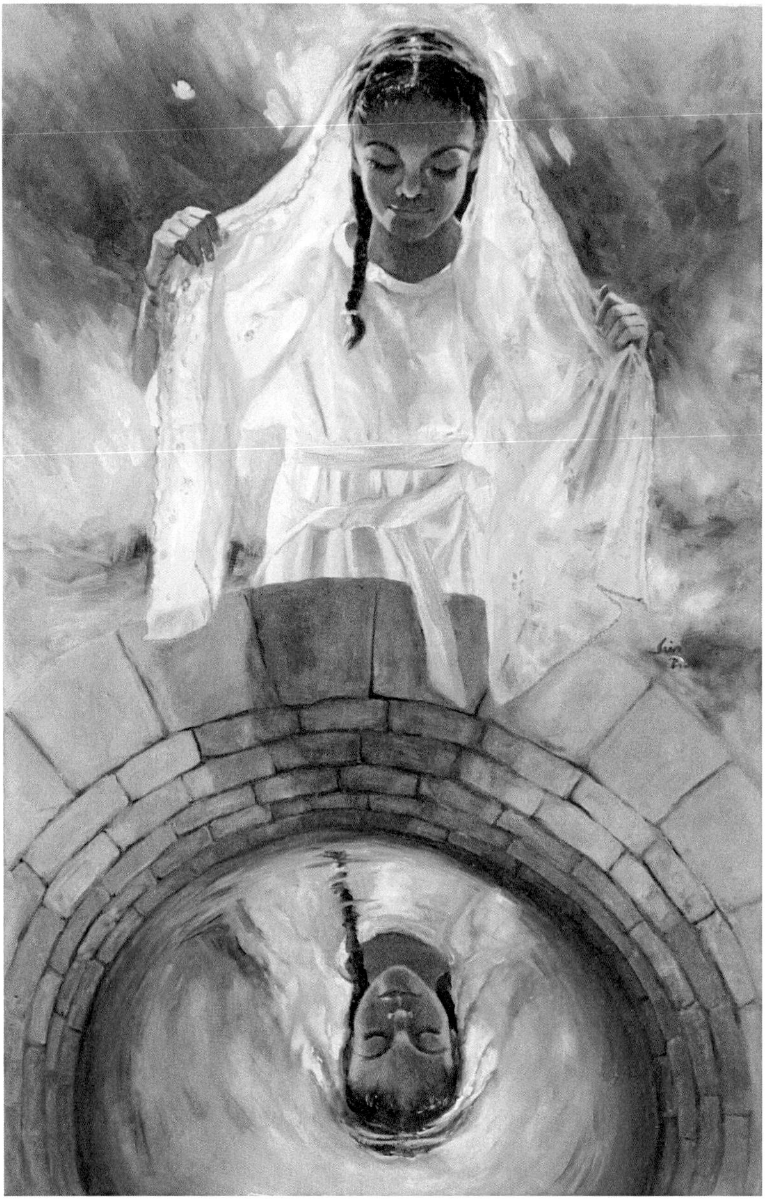

MORIAH'S SONG OF HOPE

Good night little sweet one,
Good night and say good-bye,
To evening's call of worry
And yesterday's wonder why.
Come now to the rest of night,
That only He can give.
Enter into evening's flight,
With dreams where thoughts can live.
Shed your clothes of trouble tight,
And don the dress of slumber light.
Close your eyes to daylight's woes,
And snuggle in from head to toe.
Sleep my child in sweet delight,
Though weeping now into the night.
Take my hand till morning's glow,
And there you'll find a joy to know.

DISCUSSION QUESTIONS FOR MORIAH'S WINGS

"Moriah's Wings" is a fictional story that is based on a true story told in the Bible in II Kings Chapter 5. This means some parts of the story come from the Bible and are true, but other parts are not in the Bible and have been made up.

Which of the following parts from the story are true (found in the Biblical account) and which are fictional (made up for this story)?

Naaman had a wife:

- True / Fiction

Naaman's wife was named Priscilla:

- True / Fiction

Naaman's wife was served by a girl taken captive from Israel:

- True / Fiction

The servant girl's name was Despairity:

- True / Fiction

The servant girl had a doll named Tikva:

- True / Fiction

The servant girl is renamed Moriah:

- True / Fiction

Naaman's wife can read:

- True / Fiction

Naaman developed leprosy:

- True / Fiction

The servant girl suggests Naaman should seek Elisha:

- True / Fiction

The king of Aram sent a letter with Naaman:

- True / Fiction

Naaman took gold, silver, and clothing with him:

- True / Fiction

Naaman gave the servant girl a gift:

- True / Fiction

1. Why do you think the author included fictional things in this story?

2. Do you think these details made the story more interesting?

3. We learn that Despairity's first name was Mara. What does Mara mean?

4. The lady who bought Despairity gives her a new name. What is the name she gives her?

5. What does Moriah Asha mean according to the story?
   Moriah means:
   and Asha means:

6. Why do you think the author gave her these names?

7. When the other servant girls make fun of Moriah, how does that make you feel?

8. Have you ever had someone make fun of you like that?

9. What is leprosy?

10. The Bible often tells stories of people having special dreams such as the one Moriah had. Do you think it's possible that Moriah might have had such a special dream? Why or why not?

11. At the end of the story Moriah sees the painted butterfly on her brush. How does she feel when she sees the butterfly?

12. At the end of the story, Priscilla remembers the papyrus note Moriah found in her doll and shares it with Naaman. Where are these verses found in the Bible?

13. Which part of these verses relates to what has just happened to Naaman?

29717984R00022

Made in the USA
San Bernardino, CA
16 March 2019